THE DAY PATCH
STOOD GUARD

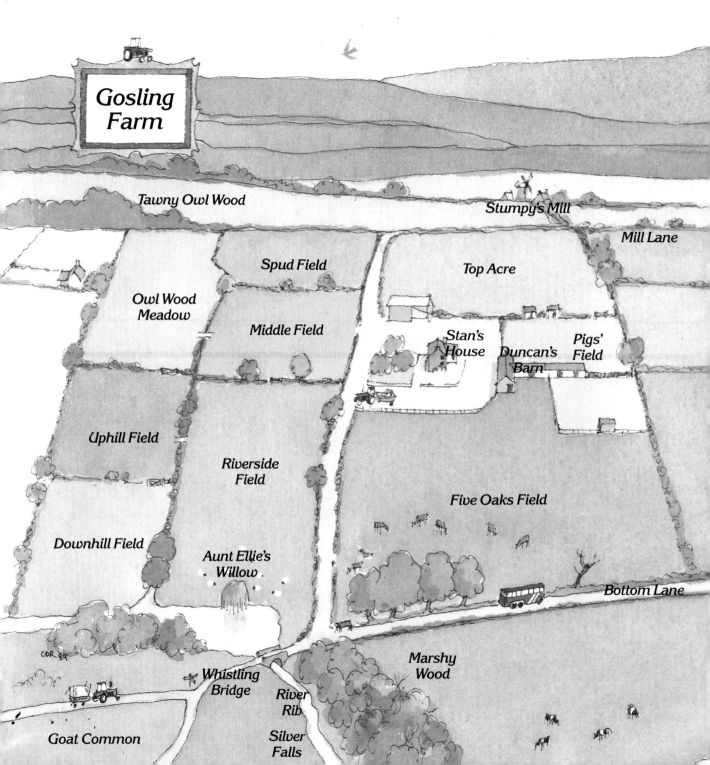

Wrigglesworth

Beech Farm

Walter's
Garage

Heronwood Lake

River Dean

For Kerrie

First published by William Collins Sons & Co Ltd 1990
First published in Picture Lions 1992

Picture Lions is an imprint of the Children's Division,
part of HarperCollins Publishers Limited,
77-85 Fulham Palace Road, Hammersmith,
London W6 8JB

Printed in Great Britain by
BPCC Hazell Books, Paulton and Aylesbury

THE DAY PATCH
STOOD GUARD

COLIN REEDER

Text by Elizabeth Laird

PictureLions

An Imprint of HarperCollins*Publishers*

A blackbird was singing loudly one bright May morning on Gosling Farm, but Stan, the farmer, didn't hear him. He was fast asleep.

A fly buzzed round his nose. Stan turned over and went on snoring. A paw scratched at his bedroom door. Patch, the young dog, wanted her breakfast.

Stan woke up with a jerk.

"Eh? Who? What's the time?" he said.

He looked at his clock. It had stopped in the night.

Stan jumped out of bed.

"Oh my goodness, I've slept in!" he said. "And there are the cows to milk, and the pigs to feed, and the eggs to collect and . . . All right, Patch, I'm coming!"

A little while later, Stan came out of his house, and hurried off to do the milking. Patch ran out after him.

The farmyard was full of exciting smells. Patch darted about, sorting them out with her nose.

A sweet, milky smell came from the new-born calves' stall. Patch pushed her wet nose under the door. It met a bigger, wetter nose on the other side. A calf was sniffing the spring air, too.

Patch jumped back, and licked her nose clean. A butterfly floated above her head. Patch jumped after it. It fluttered across to Duncan, the little red tractor. Patch liked Duncan. She curled up against his back wheel, and waited for Stan.

The sun was already high when Stan came back into the farmyard. He hitched the trailer onto the hook between Duncan's back wheels, and piled some timber into it.

"Come on Duncan," he said. "We've got to get down to the river, and mend the old bridge. Some of those planks are rotten right through."

He climbed into Duncan's cab, and Patch scrambled up after him. Then Duncan rumbled happily out of the barn and down the lane.

The lambs were happy to see the little red tractor. They jumped about on their long thin legs and bleated at him.

Patch stood up and quivered with excitement. She was a sheep dog. She knew about lambs. She'd watched her mother round them up and bring them to the shepherd. She'd show Stan that she could do it too. She jumped out of the cab.

"Hey! Patch! Careful, girl!" shouted Stan, and he stopped Duncan and climbed out of the cab too.

Patch lay down in the grass, and put her long nose on her paws. She watched Stan, ready to obey his orders. She wouldn't move a whisker until he told her to.

"Here! Patch!" called Stan.

Patch jumped up and ran to him. Stan was pleased. Patch was a sheep dog, born and bred. He could trust her not to chase the lambs, after all. He turned back to Duncan.

Then Stan got a dreadful fright.
"Hey, Duncan!" he shouted.
"Stop!"
But Duncan couldn't stop.

Stan had left his handbrake off,
and Duncan was rolling down
the hill, out of control.
Stan started running after him.
"The river!" wailed Stan.
"He's going to end up in the river!
No, he's not, he's going to crash
through the fence! No, he's not,
he's going to hit the tree!"

    With a bump, Duncan hit the tree.

The little tractor was in a sorry state. Oil dripped from his brake pipe. His front grill was bent, and his headlights were broken. The trailer had come off and turned over on its side. Curious lambs crowded round to look at him.

"Oh dear oh lor," said Stan, shaking his head. "This is a job for Walter, up at the garage."

Patch nudged Stan, and whined. Stan patted her head.

"Here, Patch, you stay and guard poor old Duncan while I go and phone Walter," said Stan.

Patch wagged her tail, and sat down by Duncan's back wheel. She looked fierce. She'd guard Duncan all right, no question of that.

It was a long time before Stan came back with Walter. Patch was very glad to see him. She thumped her feathery tail on the grass and barked with joy.

Walter inspected the trailer.

"There's not much wrong with this," he said. "You can nail those boards back yourself."

Then he looked at Duncan. This time, he shook his head.

"Hm," he said. "I can't work on him here. We'll have to hitch him to the breakdown van, and tow him back to the garage.

So Walter and Stan hooked Duncan on to the breakdown van, and they set off.

In the garage, Stan drove Duncan onto a ramp, and Walter pressed a button. The little red tractor rose into the air.

Walter peered carefully into Duncan's insides. Then he lowered Duncan down to the ground again.

"It's not too bad," he said. "Leave him here tonight, Stan, and I'll work on him tomorrow. He should be fine by the afternoon."

The two men left the garage talking busily. Patch sat down beside Duncan. Stan had told her to guard the little red tractor, and she was going to do just that.

Five minutes passed, then ten. Patch heard a car starting up outside the garage. Walter was taking Stan home! They'd been so worried about Duncan they'd forgotten all about her!

It was getting dark. Patch was scared. She wanted to go home. She whimpered, and scrambled up into Duncan's cab. She felt better there. Duncan was an old friend.

A long time later, the garage door opened. Walter came in.

"Patch!" he said. "Stan's worried sick about you. He's just called me. I promised I'd take you home. Come on now, good dog!"

He tried to pick Patch up, but she growled at him. Stan had told her to guard Duncan, and no one was going to stop her.

Walter tried again, but Patch showed her teeth. Walter laughed. "All right, you win," he said. "Stan will take you home tomorrow."

Walter brought Patch a big bowl of supper and some water. She ate and drank hungrily, then settled down happily in Duncan's cab, and fell fast asleep.

Walter started early the next day. With a clatter and a bump he drove Duncan out into the sunny garage yard, then he unscrewed the broken bits, bolted on the new bits, and soon Duncan was as good as new.

Patch lay in the sun with her ears cocked and watched Walter carefully. She was still on guard.

At last, Stan arrived.

Patch was overjoyed. She wagged her tail so hard that her back half wagged with it. Walter laughed at her.

"She's the best little guard dog I ever did see," he said.

Later, Stan drove Duncan up the road that led to Gosling Farm. He hadn't forgotten Patch this time. Her nose was poking out of the tractor's window.

A flash of blue over the river caught Stan's eye.

"A kingfisher!" he said, and pulled up by the bank.

The little bird swooped under the bridge and disappeared, but Patch's sharp eyes had spotted something else. A sleek, dark head with a fine set of whiskers was swimming downstream through the clear, clean water.

"The otter," said Stan quietly.

Patch nearly barked, but Stan laid his hand on her head.

"Quiet, girl," he said. "We don't want to frighten him."

The otter dived down into the river, and only a ripple showed where he had been. Stan turned Duncan and drove him up the lane towards the farmyard.

The sun sparkled on Duncan's new chromium grill. It shimmered on his bright new headlamps, and glinted off his polished paintwork.

The cows lifted their heads contentedly as Duncan passed Five Oaks Field, and the lambs frisked over to their gate to watch him pass. Even the mother goose, leading her goslings down to the river, stretched out her long neck and cackled at him.

Everyone was glad to see the little red tractor safe home again.

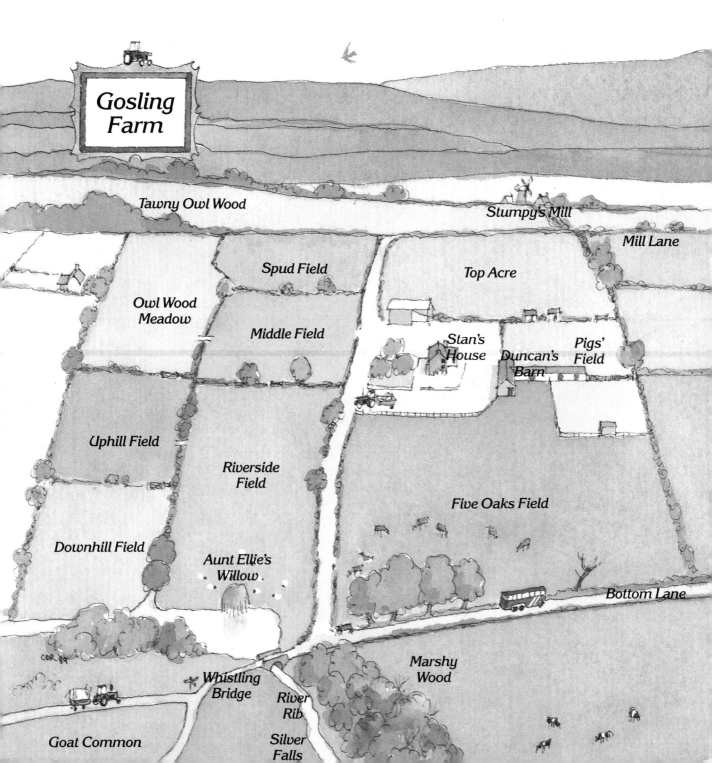

Wrigglesworth

Beech Farm

Walter's Garage

Heronwood Lake

River Dean